# night rabbits

# night rabbits

## Monica Wellington

PUFFIN BOOKS

•   FOR JEFF   •

PUFFIN BOOKS
Published by the Penguin Group
Penguin Putnam Books for Young Readers, 345 Hudson Street, New York, New York 10014, U.S.A.
Penguin Books Ltd, 27 Wrights Lane, London W8 5TZ, England
Penguin Books Australia Ltd, Ringwood, Victoria, Australia
Penguin Books Canada Ltd, 10 Alcorn Avenue, Toronto, Ontario, Canada M4V 3B2
Penguin Books (N.Z.) Ltd, 182-190 Wairau Road, Auckland 10, New Zealand

Penguin Books Ltd, Registered Offices: Harmondsworth, Middlesex, England

First published in the United States of America by Dutton Children's Books, a division of Penguin Books USA, Inc., 1995
Published by Puffin Books, a member of Penguin Putnam Books for Young Readers, 1999

1  3  5  7  9  10  8  6  4  2

LIBRARY OF CONGRESS CATALOGING-IN-PUBLICATION DATA
Wellington, Monica.
Night rabbits / Monica Wellington.
p.   cm.
Summary: Simple text and illustrations depict the nighttime activities of two young rabbits.
ISBN 0-14-055768-7
1. Rabbits—Juvenile fiction. [1. Rabbits—Fiction. 2. Night—Fiction.] I. Title.
[PZ10.3.W458Ni 1999] [E]—dc21 98-8395 CIP AC

Printed in the United States of America

Gouache, watercolors, and colored pencils were used
to create the full-color art in this book.

Day is ending
Nighttime coming
Wake up little rabbits, hop.

Rabbits in the garden eating
Nibble nibble crunch.

Noses twitching
Whiskers wiggling
Little rabbits sniff.

Owl in the night sky swooping
Beware little rabbits, scoot.

Raccoon in the cornfield rustling
Snake in the long grass slithering

Leap little rabbits, fly.

Big bear in the orchard lumbering

Thumping bumping thud.

Rabbits by the berry bushes

Tickle tickle dance.

Raindrops falling
Night storm coming
Stop little rabbits, listen.

**Thunder crashing
Lightning flashing
Quiver shiver shake.**

Red fox in the dark woods slinking
Run little rabbits, run.

# Nighttime ending
# Bright sun rising

Scurry hurry home.

Insects in the meadow humming
Little rabbits hush.

Back at last
Snuggle cuddle
Sleep little rabbits, sleep.